Bear in Love

Daniel Pinkwater   illustrated by Will Hillenbrand

WALKER BOOKS
AND SUBSIDIARIES
LONDON • BOSTON • SYDNEY • AUCKLAND

A bear lived in the woods. He had a little cave, just big enough for him.

Every morning, the bear would crawl out of his cave,
rub his eyes, stretch and feel the morning sun.
Then he would look round for something to eat.

This particular morning, the bear saw something on the flat rock in the clearing outside his cave.

"What is that?" the bear said. It was orange and long and pointy and had green bushy leaves at one end.

"It smells nice," the bear said. "It might be good to eat."
He nibbled it.

"It is crunchy. It tastes good, too! Yum!"

He went off through the woods, singing a song to himself:

"Very good, very good
Very good indeed
Very good, yum yum yum
Very good indeed."

The next morning, when the bear crawled out of his cave...

"Look! Two more of them! Two more of those crunchy things! Someone must have left them for me. I wonder who."

He went off through the woods, singing a song
to himself:

"I wonder who
I wonder who
I wonder who, hum, hum, hum
I wonder who."

The next morning, when the bear crawled out of his cave...

"Crunchy things! Three of them! I will eat two now and save one for later."

But he ate them all.

"Someone is nice to leave these for me,"
the bear thought. He went off through the
forest, singing a song to himself:

> "Someone is nice
> Someone is nice
> Very good, yum yum yum
> I wonder who."

The next morning... "What? What? What, what, what? A whole bunch of them? Someone must like me to leave these good things!"

He went off through the forest, singing a song to himself:

"*Someone must like me*
Someone is nice
Very good, yum yum yum
Someone is nice."

The bear followed some bees. He followed
them to a hollow tree. In the hollow tree,
there was a beehive.
"Honey!" the bear thought.

The bees were angry, but the bear didn't care.
He scooped out chunks of honeycomb with his
claws. He licked the honey and got all sticky with it.

"I will eat all this honey," the bear thought.
"No, not all. I will save some for ... for ...
the nice ... for the nice friend!" He went
through the woods, singing:

> *"Sticky honey*
> *Nice nice*
> *Sticky honey*
> *Nice nice."*

The bear left the honeycomb on the flat rock.
He watched from the mouth of his cave.
He wanted to see who came to the flat rock.
He wanted to see who had left him the nice things.
He wanted to see who came, and he wanted to
see the friend find the honeycomb.

But he fell asleep. When the bear woke up,
the sun was shining, the honeycomb was gone
and there was a flower on the flat rock.

"This is frustrating," thought the bear while smelling the flower. "I wonder who it is."

All day he sang a song to himself:

"*I wonder who it is*
I wonder who it is
I wonder who it is."

That night, the bear left blueberries on the rock.
He stayed just beside the rock and tried hard
not to fall asleep – but he did.

In the morning, every blueberry was gone, and there was a cookie on the rock. It was a big cookie, and it had raisins.

"This is special," the bear thought as he ate the cookie. "This is extra special." And he sang:

> "Extra special
> Extra special
> Extra special
> Extra special."

The bear went down to the road,
where he did not usually go.

He lifted a chocolate bar with only two
bites missing out of a rubbish bin and
took it to the flat rock.

"Extra special," the bear thought. He hummed and thought about what it would be like for someone to find the chocolate bar.

"Hum hum
Ha ha
Hum hum
Ha ha."

A few nights after leaving the chocolate bar with only two bites missing on the flat rock, the bear was sitting in the moonlight when he heard someone singing a beautiful song and thought he saw a shadow flit across the clearing.

The bear sang a song, and he had a feeling someone was listening.

The next night, as the bear sang a song, he saw someone peeping out from the bushes.

"You are some cute little bear," the bear said.

"And you are quite the big strong bunny!"

(You might think there would be some confusion at this point, but apparently not.)

"Those things you first left," the bear said.

"Carrots," the bunny said. "They are much favoured by bunnies."

"Imagine that," the bear said. "How did you like the chocolate bar?"

"I thought it was extra special."

"I hoped you would."

And the two of them sat side by side in the
clearing, singing songs as the sun went down.

For Jill, who is sweet and crunchy
D. P.

For Ann, who is extra special
W. H.

First published 2012 by Walker Books Ltd
87 Vauxhall Walk, London SE11 5HJ

This edition published 2014

2 4 6 8 10 9 7 5 3 1

Text © 2012 Daniel Pinkwater

Illustrations © 2012 Will Hillenbrand

The right of Daniel Pinkwater and Will Hillenbrand to be identified as author
and illustrator respectively of this work has been asserted by them in
accordance with the Copyright, Designs and Patents Act 1988

This book has been typeset in Aged

Printed in China

British Library Cataloguing in Publication Data:
a catalogue record for this book is available from the British Library

ISBN 978-1-4063-4534-6

www.walker.co.uk